KICK OFF

Andrew Fusek Peters
and Polly Peters

Evans

PLAYS WITH ATTITUDE

'To find out more about the authors, visit www.tallpoet.com

Published in 2007 by
Evans Brothers Ltd
2A Portman Mansions
Chiltern Street
London W1U 6NR

Text copyright © Andrew Fusek Peters and Polly Peters 2007

British Library Cataloguing in Publication Data

Peters, Andrew (Andrew Fusek)
    Kick off. - (Plays with attitude)
    1. Soccer teams - Great Britain - Juvenile drama
    2. Boarding schools - Great Britain - Juvenile drama
    3. Children's plays, English
    I. Title II. Peters, Polly
    822.9'14

ISBN 9780237533748

Editor: Su Swallow
Designer: Robert Walster, Big Blu Design
Printed in Malta

Cover image istockphoto.com

FOREWORD

Kick Off plays out over the course of a term at ill-fated
Diddlebury Heights High School. Not only is the school
languishing miserably at the bottom of the football league, but
it has only one term left in order to prove ownership of the very
land it stands on. Failure to do so spells certain closure and the
rampant development of the sports fields by the greedy great-
granddaughter of the school's original benefactor. Insult is
added to injury when, after a match with arch-rivals Mill Spill,
the school's historic and valuable football trophy disappears.
Morale is lower even than some of the puns featured in this
comedy-thriller! Will Diddlebury Heights ever scrape their way
back up the league? Can anything be done to foil the plans of
evil would-be developer Mrs Prodger? Who pinched the
treasured trophy? It's all to play for in a game that extends
beyond the football pitch to the very future of the school. *Kick
Off*'s fast-moving plot is set to the backdrop of pun-addicted
commentators, rapping cheerleaders, one hypochondriac coach,
and a (very) mixed boy-girl football team.

 Kick Off combines strong, individual roles with group
ensemble performance. There is scope for the imaginative
development of a range of physical theatre skills. The play also
offers a variety of challenging character monologues as well as
comic duologues. The text can be used for full-length
performances by school or youth theatre groups, or individual
scenes can be explored as stand-alone pieces during drama
lessons or youth theatre sessions. *Plays With Attitude* have been
devised to appeal especially to young performers and audiences
in Key Stage 3 and 4, and to offer a text-based framework for
developing the individual and ensemble performance skills
explored by students for course requirements.

CAST LIST

DIDDLEBURY HEIGHTS:
MR STERN: Head Teacher
MR DEXTER: Deputy Head Teacher
MR PATTERSON: PE Teacher/Football Coach
MOLEY
GREGORY
BETTS
TIM AND JIM: Commentators (note: if played by girls, change names to Queenie and Jeannie or other rhyming pair)
PUPILS/VOICES
CHEERLEADERS
MOLEY'S GANG
GREGORY'S GANG
FOOTBALL TEAM MEMBERS
CHORUS

MRS PRODGER
ARNOLD POULTEN-MOLE

MILL SPILL FOOTBALL TEAM MEMBERS
POLICE OFFICERS

Cast requirements: with very careful doubling, *Kick Off* can be performed with a minimum cast of 13. Or, it is suited to a very large cast for whole school or youth theatre production.

Act One - Scene 1

Set requires a row of stage blocks along edges of stage left and right to suggest spectator stands and to offer differentiated heights for other scenes. Blocks remain on stage throughout.

Two football commentators stand in a marked area of stage. Both hold microphones. Commentators can be either girls or boys – Tim and Jim or Queenie and Jeannie.

TIM: Beginning of the game, Jim and the pitch is empty as a new…dustbin.

JIM: The crowd is looking forward to the match! *[Looks at audience in silence for a few seconds]* Yes, the look on their faces says that anything can happen.

TIM: It's all up for grabs like a stereo from the open window of a car.

All cast except Head Teacher assemble on stage, marching on, chanting. All take places on one side in crowd formation that can double for assembly in scene 2

ALL: I'll be a Diddlebury fan, mostly, mostly!
          I'll be a Diddlebury fan, mostly, mostly yes!
          Mostly, mostly yes!
          Mostly, mostly, yes!
          I'll be a Diddlebury fan, mostly, mostly yes!

JIM: Now we just have to wait for the toss…

TIM: errr

TIM AND JIM: So let's hear from the boss! *[Both exit]*

5

Scene 2

Morning Assembly at Diddlebury Heights School. Cast move to fill central space. Head Teacher enters and mounts raised stage block. A few pupils are fidgeting about and being generally annoying.

HEAD: *[Pompous, overbearing, grandiose. He uses arms to make big gestures. Words pile up in a manner that almost causes Head to lose the thread]* Our first day of the summer term. Good morning Diddlebury Heights! Well, it's debatable how good it is but I can hardly say, 'Bad morning,' can I? No. As we face the (sadly, now inevitable) closure of this venerable, esteemed place of learning, we must nonetheless hold our heads high upon the neck of knowledge, the collarbone of creativity, the shoulder of...lamb! Where was I?

A pupil sniggers

Oh! *[Points at pupil]* Do you laugh at me, boy?

PUPIL: No Sir.

HEAD: Does that upward movement of your facial muscles indicate an impertinent grin, an insolent smirk?

PUPIL: Not at all Sir.

HEAD: *[Suddenly sinister, pulls out a pair of scissors and snips them threateningly]* Do you understand the meaning of the verbs castigate, chastise... disembowel? You do know that scissors can be used for more than just snipping...paper? Snip, snip, snip!

PUPIL: *[Very high pitched squeak]* Y...yes Sir!

HEAD: Good. *[Replaces scissors in pocket]* I'm so pleased that you are with me on this. I think you can stop being such a whining...I mean...shining wit, now! Perhaps we can leave the potential surgical procedure for another time, hmm?

PUPIL: Whatever you say, Sir!

HEAD: Exactly. Whatever I say, eh? Me being the Head, as it were, and you simply part of the body, of pupils. Me - the captain. You - the team-players of the beautiful game. Ah yes, and while we're on the subject of balls...

More sniggering

[Head stares until pupils are silent. Points at one of the trouble makers. Sarcastic] Ha! Ha! Ha! Foot...balls. You can stay in after school and have a distended extension...err...extensive retention...mmmm... punishment! Now where was I? Yes, Diddlebury Heights. We may appear to have fallen behind somewhat in the league, but we were great once - players, strikers, scorers: feet gliding down the pitch like swans and oh! When those feet struck upon the ball, how it soared into the sky, an unstoppable comet! Yes, we were the originals, the winners, the true heirs to: The Poulten and Mole's Potted Shrimp Cup!

Sudden blackout, spotlight on large trophy cup held aloft. Chorus chant, quietly at first, growing louder

The Poulten and Mole's Potted Shrimp Cup!
The Poulten and Mole's Potted Shrimp Cup!
The Poulten and Mole's Potted Shrimp Cup!

The spotlit cup is carried by figure in black. As chorus (ie the assembled cast on stage) chant, they split into two groups, one on either side of stage, like football teams

CHORUS GROUP 1: Back in nineteen thirty-one

CHORUS GROUP 2: When the league had just begun

CHORUS GROUP 1: Our lads were mean

CHORUS GROUP 2: And fast and quick

CHORUS GROUP 1: Train 'em hard

CHORUS GROUP 2: And make 'em slick

CHORUS GROUP 1: Whack that leather

CHORUS GROUP 2: When we scored

CHORUS GROUP 1: What a sound

CHORUS GROUP 2: When that crowd

BOTH CHORUS GROUPS: *[Shouting]* **ROARED**

CHORUS GROUP 1: Climb the league!

CHORUS GROUP 2: Yes, get on up!

CHORUS GROUP 1: The Poulten and Mole's

CHORUS GROUP 2: Potted Shrimp Cup!

CHORUS GROUP 1: The Poulten and Mole's Potted Shrimp Cup!

CHORUS GROUP 2: The Poulten and Mole's Potted Shrimp Cup!

BOTH GROUPS: **The Poulten and Mole's Potted Shrimp Cup!**

Blackout. Chorus step back to previous positions as pupils. Lights up. Head now holds cup in hand, caressing it like a pet

HEAD: *[Reading inscription on the cup]* 'This trophy, donated to Diddlebury Heights by Arnold Poulten-Mole the First, shall stand for all time as a record of good deeds on the football pitch.' Yes! In 1931 this school was at the very pinnacle of the League Table.

Winners! Celebrated by the benefactor of the school with this stupendous cup. Look at that beauty, that workmanship. It is our most prized and valuable possession. Let it inspire you to reach for glory once again. So come. We must cast off misfortune and lift up the future with the forklift of the past! We have one last chance to regain our reputation! One last term. We shall fight them on the pitches!

And by the way, good luck in the friendly with Mill Spill this afternoon: a little warm up for the league games later this term, eh? Do break a leg (metaphorically speaking). Glory! Etcetera, etcetera, etcetera. Dismissed. *[Waves hands as if suddenly preoccupied]*

Pupils become a scrum, milling around as they gather themselves. They begin a strident marching rhythm with feet as they break into three smaller, milling groups

GROUP 1

1:     Who cares about a rubbish old cup?

2:     We haven't won a game all year.

3:     Don't know what the Head's got to be so cheerful about.

GROUP 2

4:     Cheerful? You mean bonkers!

5:     Bonkers? That man is a few studs short of a boot!

6:     Anyway, what's the point in playing to win?

7:     The school will still be closed at the end of term.

Group 3

8:     I can't believe they're going to build over the fields.

9:     Who cares? It's a dump anyway. Good riddance, I say.

10:     Yeah. There's more to life than football.

All crowd on stage fall suddenly silent and stare threateningly at Voice 10

All: *[Very loud]* **What?**

10:     It's just a figure of speech.

All: *[Incredulous]* **A figure of speech?**

All take one step towards Voice 10

10:     *[A little concerned and scared, but still defensive]* It's only a game!

Betts: *[Steps forward]* Only! A game! *[Nods to the crowd]*

A member of the crowd raises a football behind Voice 10's head and 'hits' Voice 10 over the head with it. S/he falls down and dies in highly exaggerated, slow and painful way. As Voice 10 lies down, one of chorus pulls out big red scarf or handkerchief from inside Voice 10's collar to signify blood. Betts steps forward and places foot on body as if in triumph

Betts: And there's more to football than life. You, my boy/girl, prove the point!

Voice 1 lifts up red scarf and wipes hands on it, as if bloodied, then drops it

Red card! Very, very red! Take him/her away!

Body of Voice 10 is dragged off stage. All except Head exit

Scene 3

Head carries two chairs centre stage and sits with feet on second chair. He elaborately blows nose into large handkerchief and mimes re-arranging imaginary items very precisely on desk in front. Hums something suitably traditional/upstanding to himself. 'Knock' on door from off stage.

HEAD: Who is it?

DEXTER: *[Off stage]* It's Dexter, Mr Stern.

HEAD: *[Bellows]* Dexter Who?

Chorus from off stage sings 'Dexter' halls with boughs of holly, tra la la la la, la-la-la-la!

DEXTER: *[Shouts]* Shut…Up! *[Opens mimed door forcefully, slams it]* Me! Mr Dexter! Your Deputy Head!

HEAD: Ah, you. Do sit down.

This whole scene uses chairs in a sequence of movements, according to stage directions, indicating status. It requires tightly choreographed moves to create a visual struggle for power and one-upmanship. The words must be spoken as though ignoring the actions being played out

DEXTER: *[Sits down]* We really must come up with an action plan.

HEAD: *[Stands up, towering over Deputy Head]* Action! That's the ticket.

DEXTER: *[Stands up, facing Head]* Talk will get us nowhere. Where do you stand on this issue?

HEAD: *[Stands on chair]* We have to make a stand! One last shot at glory before our dear Diddlebury Heights disappears beneath a wave of new development. Besides, Patterson is an excellent coach.

DEXTER: *[Stands on chair to meet Head eye to eye]* I don't think you understand the severity of the situation. Have you *seen* Patterson teach?

HEAD: A fine, upstanding, team-leader. Let me find you a more comfortable chair. *[He clicks fingers and a smaller chair is slid on to stage – a primary school chair, or staffroom seat – anything that's lower than the Head's]*

DEXTER: That's very kind of you.

Both move to sit down. Deputy looks at both chairs before sitting down on the new chair. Before the Head tries to sit down in one of the original chairs, Deputy clicks fingers and an even smaller chair/stool is slid onto stage and the two larger chairs are removed

DEXTER: Do take the weight off your feet Mr Stern.

Head sits, now lower than Deputy

I've had a thought. This new boy, Rodgers - goes by the name of Moley - comes highly recommended. Won all sorts of cups at his old place, Bestminster.

HEAD: A strange move to make, is it not? From public school to...here! And so close to the end of dear old Diddlebury.

DEXTER: He tells us his mother had to go abroad to look after a sick relative and didn't have enough money to keep up his school fees. Apparently he's staying nearby with an old friend of the family, just until the summer holidays. Then he'll join his mum. Anyway that's not the point. The most important thing is that he sounds like a pro in the making. As you said, it's our last chance to go down in glory. Make him captain and we might strike lucky. What do you think?

HEAD: I think…I think that chair won't do much good for your back. Let me get you another. I insist. *[Clicks fingers, and a toddler-size chair or car seat is slid on to stage, picked up by the head and placed next to Deputy. Deputy tries to sit on/in it. Head is now higher than Deputy]* As the Chair of the football committee, I must respond to crisis. Let me share my inspiration with you. There is a new pupil, young Moley. Do you know of him?

DEXTER: *[Incredulous]* Yes!

HEAD: Yes indeed! The finest, fastest, most fleet feet we are likely to have the honour of seeing here at Diddlebury Heights. Perhaps if we sack the current captain, who has led us to nothing but dismal disaster, and substitute this young whippersnapper, we might have one last claim to the cup!

DEXTER: What an original idea! I wish I'd thought of it myself! *[Clicks fingers and a dolls' house chair is thrown from off stage into his hands]* You really are a most brilliant Chair! Here, try this for size, I insist! *[He places doll's chair on ground.*

Head looks down at it before carefully attempting to squat on top of it, so that Deputy now looks down at Head

DEXTER: *[Aside to audience]* And as usual, I'm the one who'll get things done. One more match this afternoon with the old team. Oh dear. Then…new training regime, sort out Patterson and work on Moley. We'll leave our boss here to tinker with his toys. Nothing changes.

Blackout. Both exit

As an alternative to the use of ever smaller chairs, this scene could be performed using the stage blocks at each side, with both characters climbing higher by stacking up the blocks.

Scene 4

Commentators enter.

JIM: And the Deputy's got it in the bag. A nifty bit of footwork, making the Head think it was his idea,

TIM: when Dexter was controlling the ball all along,

JIM: like a rabid dog…on a leash. Could this be the man of the match?

TIM: I think it could be, Jim. I think it could. But what's all this talk about game over, school closing?

JIM: Well Tim, it sure does look like a poor result for unlucky old Diddlebury. Seems they've never found the legal papers to prove they own the very grounds we're standing on.

TIM: Really Jim?

JIM: Oh, they've searched all right. Turned the place inside out. But without those documents…

TIM: It's an own goal for the Diddleys, and a sweepstake for some lucky winner.

Exit

Scene 5

Mrs Prodger enters. She is the great-granddaughter of Arnold Poulten-Mole Esquire, who originally endowed the school with the cup and also the land. She is the prospective developer, and, in the absence of the legal documents proving otherwise, she appears to be the legal heir to the Poulten-Mole estate, including all the fields round the school and the site the school is built on.

MRS PRODGER: *[Addresses and harangues audience. Doesn't stand still, paces like a cat]* Good old Great-Grandad – spotted a gap in the market. The Victorian well-to-do must have their seafood and he was happy to supply Poulten and Mole's Potted Shrimp.

Enter character of Arnold Poulten-Mole. He walks about silently, dressed in old-fashioned clothing

But then the old fool gave his money away. Do-gooding makes me sick. He endows the local school with land and a stupid, little cuppy-wuppy. And why the generosity? All for the sake of his true love: the kicking round of a muddy, inflated cow-skin. Football! Pah! *[Spits on ground]* How could he have betrayed his loyal, loving family? Apparently there were *deeds* or some legal flim-flammery! Oh! Perish the thought. *[She looks very worried and pretends to weep then pauses suddenly and cheers up]* Ah, but where are those papers now? Did they turn up, since Mr Poulten-Mole came to a sudden end? No! And if I ever get my hands on them then…*[Mimes striking a match]* Whoosh! Just a little puff of smoke my dears.

So who now stands to inherit? My cousin Eddie, feeling a bit flat since the incident with a steamroller? My former husband? We know how dangerous cliffs can be. Aunty Doris? What an unlucky little outing it was to the mushy pea factory. She fell. Drowned. *[Pause]* May she rest...in...peas. That only leaves...why I think...it's me! Yes me! Me! **Me!** Prudence Prodger. *[Dances round]* In the memory of those I mourn, it is my duty to make a mint! And turn this godforsaken dump into a multi-mega casino! By the end of this term and through my plotting, ahem, I mean good fortune, the land that Piddlebury Heights is built on will revert to its rightful owner! *[She stalks off leaving Arnold Poulten-Mole walking slowly round stage with walking stick]*

ARNOLD: I love this game with all me 'eart. So what if I made a mint? Hardly going to retire and sip champagne. Not me. Nah! I ploughed my green stuff in the ground and watched it grow into...a school...fit for sporting glory. And my cup, what a silver beauty, eh? Should impress those who laughed at me when I was a young 'un. But the thing is, you never know who's gonna try and pinch the fruit of yer hard-earned labours. So let me tell you a secret. I've 'id them deeds, good n' proper to keep them safe. And oh, what a hidey hole, a perfect goal. You see, I put them... *[As he's about to give it away, he stumbles over a small obstruction on the stage which represents the edge of a long drop. Lights drop so he is only just visible]* Aaaahhhhhhhhhhhhhhhhhhhh! *[He falls to ground in slow motion and voice off stage shouts THUMP as he lands. Member of chorus enters to drag body off stage and speaks before removing body]*

CHORUS MEMBER: What a spectacular own goal. Two hundred feet down an ancient mine shaft! He was in bits…literally. And that, I'm afraid, was the end of Arnold Poulten-Mole the First.

Exit, dragging body

Scene 6

Commentators enter.

JIM: And the away team,

TIM: captained by Mrs Prudence Prodger is trouncing poor Diddlebury Heights.

JIM: My heart weeps, Tim

TIM: Like a wounded onion, Jim.

JIM: Her ancestor will be turning in his grave,

TIM: Like a pig on a spit.

JIM: The lawyers on defense don't stand a chance against her.

TIM: She plays it dirty

JIM: as an unwashed armpit.

TIM: She's bad.

JIM: She's foul.

TIM: She's heading up the pitch.

JIM: And who will pay the penalty?

Exit

Scene 7

Enter Diddlebury Heights team (all boys) and coach Patterson. Patterson, a hypochondriac, wears woolly hat, scarf wound tightly round neck and multiple layers of clothing. He jumps up and down, shivering. Team gather in circle around him with Gregory, the current team captain.

PATTERSON: Righto everyone. Last session before the game this afternoon. I'd like to introduce our new team member Paul Rodgers. He's just joined the school for a term before he heads off abroad, but we've heard good things about him.

MOLEY: Thank you. Glad to be here. Oh and it's Moley, if that's OK. No one calls me Paul except my mum!

Other team members nod knowingly

PATTERSON: Bit of a nip in the air this morning, so get those warm woolly hats on.

All pull hats from pockets, preferably a motley selection of unfashionable offerings and put them on. Patterson coughs

Lungs not quite up to scratch today. But mustn't worry, eh. If they diagnose pneumonia early, they can treat it. Can't they?

TEAM: Yes!

PATTERSON: *[Coughs pathetically again]* Oh good. So this won't kill me then?

TEAM: No Mr Patterson!

PATTERSON: Phew. That's a relief. Right, begin with some gentle jogging on the spot.

They start to jog

Remember, if you do get short of breath, take a little rest - or a long rest. Don't over-exert yourselves. Make sure you bend the knees at exactly the right angle! I don't want you suffering arthritis in later years, like me. Oooh my poor knees. That's it. Good. Now we'll practise throwing the ball to each other - carefully. *[He brings out small tennis ball or even ping-pong ball. The team throw and catch it, exchanging questioning glances]* I was rather concerned about the health and safety implications of using a real ball - sprained wrists, bruised shoulders, not to mention the bacteria carried in the mud. Carry on now. What is it Gregory?

GREGORY: But Sir, if we don't use a real football, how are we ever going to learn?

PATTERSON: *[Put out]* Hmm. An interesting question from the team captain. However, this is only a practice session, stupid. Like the ball, it's not the real thing, hmmpf! But, in consideration of your feedback, if you really insist, we'll use a real ball for the passing. I have to say though that this pitch concerns me. The greenery is dangerous! *[Patterson bends to pick up imaginary blade of grass]* They are called blades for a reason, you know. *[Cuts self]* Ow! Oooooh! Help. I'm...bleeding.

Team gather round. He clutches finger and falls to ground

Do you think they'll have to...amputate?

TEAM: No! You'll be fine!

PATTERSON: You'll mean I'll live?

All nod

> Thank goodness. It just proves my point. Look after those limbs. Now, plastic bags at the ready. And on!

All pull carrier bags from pockets and place over trainers.

> There! That should stop those nasty blades of grass doing you an injury.

GREGORY: But Mr Patterson…this is…

PATTERSON: Don't interrupt, Gregory! Listen and learn. Never underestimate the power of a pep-talk. *[Clears throat dramatically]* Diddlebury Heights! I believe in you! This afternoon, give it your best shot, but be careful. Take on the opposition. However, if tackled, please step out of the way, as laundering of kit costs a fortune. And last, but not least, go for goal - but do mind the hamstrings and avoid slippy patches!

Whole team freezes with look of derision

PLAYER: *[Comes forward and digs imaginary hole. Points]* Hole! *[Mimes planting grass seed. Points]* Grass seed! *[Points down at hole as team point at Patterson and say]*

TEAM: **GRASS-HOLE!**

Exit

Scene 8

Football match between Diddlebury Heights and Mill Spill. Lights go up on the two commentators. The two teams face each other, stage left and stage right. This scene can be performed in a number of ways. As the commentators talk through the progress of the match, the players can create a sequence of linked tableaux to depict key moments. Or the scene can be choreographed as a dance or mimed in slow-motion sequences. Alternatively, the commentators can observe and respond to the audience as though they are playing the match. Commentators need to work on timing for exaggerating the dreadful puns and over-the-top similes and observations. Note that all Mill Spill's names are James Bond baddies.

TIM: And Mill Spill win the toss. Diddlebury's captain tries to shake hands, but Goldfinger, the Mill Spill skipper is having none of it.

JIM: Bad form, that is, eh Tim?

TIM: Yes Jim. Mill Spill drive it deep into the other half,

JIM: Diddlebury struggling to keep up. The keeper looks nervous, as he should be.

TIM: Jaws takes possession, gets his teeth into it, biting deep down the line into enemy territory.

JIM: Backheels it to Goldfinger, comfortable with the ball, look at him move!

TIM: It's like sliding on silverware.

JIM: That boy is a jewel in the rough.

TIM: And where are Diddlebury now? Their back four are scattered like cocoa pops,

JIM: with Mill Spill the cereal killers.

TIM: Oooh that was nasty. Mr Big…

JIM: and he is a giant haystack, a muscle mountain,

TIM: has squashed Gregory, the Diddlebury captain. The ref's blown his whistle.

JIM: I think he's blown his top.

TIM: Mr Big gets shown the yellow ticket

JIM: and gives a very interesting hand signal behind the ref's back in response.

BOTH: Hmm!

TIM: He's awarded a free kick. Gregory is stretchered off and Moley to substitute.

Short scene spotlighting Moley and Gregory as they pass each other. Gregory grabs Moley by the hand as he's carried off

GREGORY: I can't believe I've been *sat* on from a great height.

MOLEY: Pretty foul, mate. Don't worry. I'll sort them out.

GREGORY: Cheers. Give it your best shot. My lads are good, but they need direction. I trust you.

MOLEY: Leave it to me.

GREGORY: *[Smiles weakly]* Good man.

Match resumes

TIM: Moley takes his time, weighs up the options and…

JIM: oh my, the ball flies through the air

TIM: like an acrobatic kitten. It's up the pitch and Diddlebury are waiting for it.

JIM: Moley catches up and oh, what a lovely stepover. Kleb's been nutmegged!

TIM: And Moley's zipping up the grass

JIM: making mountains out of molehills.

TIM: Gives it a tap

JIM: like a footballing tap-dancer...

TIM: Ohhhh!

JIM: Bounces off the crossbar

TIM: like a baby from the bonnet of a car.

JIM: Mill Spill breathe a sigh of relief as Blofeld scoops it up.

TIM: To Zorin now. That boy will take over the world one day.

JIM: Spoons it over the top,

TIM: like milk into a bowl of cereal.

JIM: Snap, crackle and Scaramanga climbs into the air, oh yes! Pop goes the header!

TIM: Straight into the back of the net.

JIM: What a goal.

TIM: One nil to Mill Spill.

JIM: Let's rewind and see that goal again.

Players go into reverse as commentator presses rewind on a remote control. When the moment is played again, it is performed in slow motion. Voices slow down too. As the keeper misses the ball, the groan needs to be deep, slow and extremely drawn out

KEEPER: I...waannnt...myyy...muummmyyy!

TIM: There goes the whistle for half-time.

JIM: Time really flew by there,

TIM: like a spoon into a sink full of washing-up.

JIM: And Diddlebury are covered in the soapsuds of

TIM AND JIM: shame!

Both groups huddle round managers discussing tactics, eating imaginary oranges, taking drinks etc. Patterson wraps scarves round his team, gives them hot-water bottles etc, checks their temperatures with thermometers. Whistle goes

TIM: And Mill Spill are not pussyfooting around anymore.

JIM: From the benches, it's supersub,

TIM: Drax!

JIM: Short for Dracula, do you think?

TIM: Could be, Jim. All I know is this guy is fang-tastic.

JIM: Dead fast, Tim.

TIM: I'd stake my life on this guy's talent. I'd bet my onions on him.

JIM: Oh, I think Diddlebury are piddling themselves.

TIM: Or Piddlebury are diddling themselves?

JIM: It could be, Tim.

TIM: But he's making mincemeat of the defence, as his foot stabs the ball,

JIM: murdering the opposition – oh what's that?

A foul is committed

TIM: The ref missed it. Diddlebury's midfield striker blown away.

JIM: Was that a punch or an assassination?

TIM: Drax doesn't care as

JIM: he snipes it up the back line,

TIM: shoots, and

JIM: the bullet strikes home!

TIM: Poor keeper! Didn't know what hit him.

JIM: It's a gory mess.

Whistle blows

TIM: Game over!

JIM: And Diddlebury have failed.

TIM: Tears are flooding onto the pitch

JIM: like a broken down dishwasher.

TIM: For a so-called friendly, Jim

JIM: I'd hate to see the real thing, Tim.

BOTH: Oh dearie, dearie me!

Mill Spill run a victory lap of honour while Diddlebury look downcast. They hurl chants and taunts as they leave the stage

MILL SPILL TEAM: We'll lift the cup,
          We'll lift the cup
          We'll lift that cup
          From you, right up!
          Losers! Losers! Don't you see-
          We'll take the cup in victory!
          We'll take the cup in victory!

Exit Diddlebury, despondently

Scene 9 part 1

Enter Deputy Head and Patterson.

DEXTER: Ah, there you are Patterson. A word, if you please.

PATTERSON: If it's about the match, I blame the grass. Very slippy today.

DEXTER: Yes, life's a pitch, isn't it. How are you feeling today?

PATTERSON: Now that you mention it, there's a spot on my nose I'm rather worried about. Will you have a look at it?

DEXTER: *[Peers closely, in expert manner]* Hmm. Interesting.

PATTERSON: Interesting? It's red, and sore and I thought of going to the doctor, but he threatened to cut off my…prescriptions last time I went, even though it was only my fourth visit in three days.

DEXTER: Red *and* sore, did you say?

PATTERSON: *[Very worried]* What do you mean?

DEXTER: Look, it's probably benign. It's just that I've been reading on the net about something. But I don't want to alarm you…yet.

PATTERSON: *[Alarmed]* Alarm?

DEXTER: Let's just put both our minds at rest. Do you have any other symptoms?

PATTERSON: Tired, worried, concerned about my chilblains, aching hips, a slight buzzing in my ears, and a very itchy toenail on my left foot.

DEXTER: *[Interrupts]* The left foot? Are you sure it's not the right?

Patterson shakes head

No. I don't believe it. It's too much of a coincidence.

PATTERSON: What?

DEXTER: Nothing. No, I'm sure you'll be fine. I mean, it's a very rare condition.

PATTERSON: [*Almost squeaking in terror*] Rare?

DEXTER: The fatality rate is only fifty per cent…

PATTERSON: Fatality? *Only?*

DEXTER: But you know the World Wide Web is no substitute for sound medical advice…except in this case. The epidemic has rather taken the World Health Organisation by surprise. Have you heard of it?

PATTERSON: [*Gulps*] Computers not really my thing.

DEXTER: [*Quietly*] I know. [*Louder*] AHSWS. Advanced Hypochondriac Snivelling Whinge Syndrome.

PATTERSON: Oh help.

DEXTER: I know. It must come as a shock. Do take a seat. [*Clicks fingers. Camp bed is pushed on to stage. Pushes Patterson on to it and tucks blanket over*] The only cure is extreme bed rest: at least three months. All sporting activity is a no-no of course.

PATTERSON: But how can the team go on without me?

DEXTER: Dear man, they'll miss your amazing abilities. We will simply try to be brave and soldier on.

PATTERSON: If you think it's for the best.

DEXTER: [*Mask of concern slips, menacingly*] I do…but don't you worry. Just take the rest of the term off. Keep warm. Keep well. Keep away from the pitch.

Patterson is pushed offstage

Scene 9 part 2

Deputy on stage. Moley enters as if walking down a corridor. Chorus enter and mill round silently on way to lessons. Deputy and Moley walk among them stopping at intervals to talk.

MOLEY: Hello, Mr Dexter.

DEXTER: Good to see you Moley. Nice playing today. Shame about your strike. A couple of centimetres and it would have been in the net.

MOLEY: That's very kind of you, Sir.

DEXTER: *[Falls in beside him as they walk around the stage]* Tell me now, why do they call you Moley?

MOLEY: Oh that. Too many rhyming nicknames for the surname Rodger.

DEXTER: Oh? *[Thinking]* Bodger, codger, dodger, lodger, tod… Ah! I see!

MOLEY: Known as Moley because - well, I'm fast and close to the ground, just like a mole, you never see me coming!

DEXTER: I see…anyway, to the point. The thing is, it seems Patterson has taken ill.

MOLEY: I'm sorry to hear that.

DEXTER: Are you really?

MOLEY: Er. No. Man's a twit Sir. Doesn't know his…ahem… from his elbow, Sir.

DEXTER: Precisely. I've decided to take on his commitments, having fallen in love with the beautiful game myself.

MOLEY: Do you still play then?

Chorus begin to drift slowly to the sides, leaving Dexter and Moley centre stage

DEXTER: I used to…a long time ago. But back to the point. A few changes need to be made. I'm thinking of demoting Gregory.

MOLEY: But he's a fine captain Sir.

DEXTER: He's been ruined by Patterson! Never been allowed to use his initiative. I ask again, do you really mean that?

MOLEY: Well…

DEXTER: You seem to inspire courage in the team.

MOLEY: Do I?

DEXTER: They've taken to you. They look up to you.

MOLEY: You think so? Even after only one game? *[Takes out pocket mirror, sighs as he looks into it, preens]*

DEXTER: I do, and for that reason, and also so we can actually start winning the occasional game, I'd like you to consider becoming captain.

MOLEY: Little old me? Moi? Wow!

DEXTER: And that's precisely what we want the crowd to say when you score next time.

MOLEY: When you put it like that…

DEXTER: I do. So, thank you for taking up the mantle…

Betts and Gregory burst in, gabbling, upset. With each interjection, chorus create tableaux of shocked reactions to the news

BETTS: It's gone.

GREGORY: Vanished!

BETTS: Departed!

GREGORY: Disappeared.

DEXTER: What? Our good fortune? Tell me something new!

BETTS: No, it's much worse than that.

GREGORY: It's the end.

DEXTER: Patterson is actually dead? Hallelujah!

BETTS: No Sir. The cup: Poulten and Mole's Potted Shrimp

BOTH: It's gone!

Sudden blackout, spotlight on cup held aloft as before and chant, in background, growing louder from chorus

CHORUS: The Poulten and Mole's Potted Shrimp Cup!
          The Poulten and Mole's Potted Shrimp Cup!
          The Poulten and Mole's Potted Shrimp...*[at this point the cup is covered with a black cloth and vanishes! Chorus finish sentence, very despondent and quiet]*...Cup...

DEXTER: Goodness, the Head will be upset. Still, no point crying over spilt tea etc.

BETTS: But Sir, that cup is the heart of the school.

DEXTER: Hmm. Bit of cliché, my girl. It's a piece of metal, beaten by a few hammers into the shape of a vessel with some scribbling on it.

GREGORY: How can you say that?

DEXTER: Pardon?

GREGORY: How can you say that...Sir?

DEXTER: By opening and closing my mouth. Anyway, might galvanize the team, what? Anger, motivation...all good stuff.

BETTS: But we don't even know who took it.

DEXTER: More important things to think about right now. I have news. This little defeat today will not hold us back. The team has a new coach: me, and we are going to make some changes.

GREGORY: Excellent! About time.

DEXTER: We need to re-jig the team, get the players on their feet, work the strategies...

GREGORY: I'm with you all the way sir.

DEXTER: Good. The captain of the team needs support.

GREGORY: Too right.

DEXTER: So, I hope you'll be happy to step down in favour of our new rising star. I present your new team captain - Moley.

GREGORY: *[Totally shocked]* No-ooo!

Exit Gregory, Betts and Dexter

Scene 10

Chorus step forward to perform this scene in Chinese whispers style. Each spoken line is passed on to the next person who reacts in exaggerated fashion before passing on the next bit of the story.

CHORUS:

1:      It was after the so-called friendly game,

2:      Gregory limped in with a face full of shame:

3:      Screaming and shouting, mad as a hatter.

4:      They followed to find out what was the matter.

5:      Discovered outside the library,

6:      a cabinet full of history,

7:      glass door swinging wide

8:      and the only shelf inside

ALL: empty!

9:      Suspicion went up in a shout!

10:     Who are the thieves? We have no doubt!

11:     One-nil

12:     to Mill-Spill!

13:     Bad enough to lose our luck,

14:     they've pushed our faces in the muck.

15:     Fouling, stealing, dirty kickers -

16:     what a stinking, set of nickers!

Chorus suddenly freeze as a police whistle sounds. Several policemen/women enter auditorium and begin questioning members of audience. Chorus move to sides and sit, as though waiting to be interviewed. This is a short, improvised scene with opportunities to rifle through handbags, interrogate and playfully intimidate audience members and to generally be officious officers of the law. Finally, after another whistle blast, one of the PCs clambers up on stage to make an announcement reading from notebook

PC: Ahem! Ahem! Having…er cordoned off the search area, conducted exhaustive interviews and checked out the concrete hardness of dodgy alibis we are able to ascertain with complete certainty that

A} The Poulten and Mole's Cup is not located presently where it was.

B} That this means it is indeed, according to our dedicated detectives, at this very moment, definitely…elsewhere.

And C} That our continuing lines of enquiry will lead to a successful summing up of our conclusion at some point yet to be determined by our determined and resourceful team. Thank you. That's all. *[Exit]*

Chorus crowd mill around. The end of this scene can either be performed using the text below or, it can be improvised. If improvising, performers need to devise ever madder and more improbable theories as to who took the cup and why

CHORUS:

1:       So much for the police. They haven't got a clue… maybe the cup suffered spontaneous combustion!

2:       Shamed by Diddlebury's rubbish performance…

3:       And the door was blown wide in the explosion!

4:       That would explain it:

5: Or the cook could have taken it, desperate for a mixing bowl.

6: Or a loaded mouse in need of an expensive, portable swimming pool.

7: What about someone in the audience, eh? [*All stop and stare out into the audience*]

8: Nah! Look at them! They wouldn't have the guts!

9: It could be the missing part of a giant's brassiere – 57D Cup! [*Name any suitable model*] eat your heart out.

10: A fashion victim trying out the latest headgear.

11: A helmet for extreme sports.

ALL: **CLANG!!!!**

1: It was invited on a chat show.

2: It was offered a bit part in Match Of The Day:

3: "Poulten, what do you think of [*Name any current famous player*] playing? "Well, bear in mind I'm only a silver-gilt cup, but in my opinion, he needs to <u>handle</u> the ball better!"

4: It ran away with a lovely, young mug.

5: And they gave birth to lots of little egg cups. What a lovely cup-ple.

ALL: **Ahhhhh!**

7: So many possible endings. How about a positive one:

8: Got retrained to provide a silver-lining for clouds.

All exit

Scene 11

Moley and team, including Betts, meet to discuss tactics. Moley sits on chair with a stage block behind. Team use stage blocks as benches. Gregory is still in team, but murmurs dissent. As the scene opens, Dexter stands on stage block behind Moley like a puppet master. Team do not seem to see him. He moves Moley's body into various positions and gestures. Moley seems unsure at first, trying to copy or resist the moves.

DEXTER: This is the way I see it. *[Lifts up Moley's left hand and points finger]*

MOLEY: Errr…this is the way I see it.

DEXTER: We gotta get our act

MOLEY: We gotta get our act

DEXTER AND MOLEY: *[Dexter lifts Moley's fist up and thumps it onto Moley's other, spread palm]* TOGETHER!

MOLEY AND DEXTER: I'm running the show now! *[Dexter nods Moley's head]* So, if you don't like it, you can leave. *[Dexter folds Moley's arms]*

DEXTER: The cup may have been stolen from us.

MOLEY: The cup may have been stolen…

DEXTER: *[Gets carried away. Forgets about Moley]* Those visiting soccer hooligans *may* have left our school with rather *more* than just our tattered self-respect. But let that only serve us to teach them a lesson. Our thirst for revenge will drive us…

Moley's facial expressions show him trying to begin speaking throughout this speech. Finally, he moves just his head to look up at Dexter. Moley's next line cuts across the end of Dexter's

    ...to achieve great things on the field!

MOLEY: [*Stage whispers through side of mouth*] Psssst. What was the beginning bit again?

DEXTER: What? Oh, never mind! [*Speaks slowly and lifts both of Moley's arms out to the side in a gesture of welcome*] Are you with me?

MOLEY: [*Turns to Dexter, hisses*] That's my line!

DEXTER: Sorry! Go on.

MOLEY: [*Shrugs Dexter's hands off*] Are you with me?

Dexter folds arms and sits unobtrusively to observe

GREGORY: We haven't got much choice, have we?

MOLEY: No, you don't. And your idea of running the team was to run it down.

GREGORY: Oh very clever.

MOLEY: Let's face it mate, you're obviously confused – there is a difference between the words Athletic and P-athetic.

GREGORY: [*Standing up*] I don't have to stand for this.

MOLEY: But you are. I would like to help you out, Greg. Which way did you come in?

This gets a few laughs from some team members. Betts seems confused by Moley's viciousness, but others smirk as Gregory storms off with a few of his mates, also disgruntled

MOLEY: That's that settled then. We need fresh blood. Betts – you explain.

Couple of team members murmur

What's she to do with it? She's only a cheerleader.

BETTS: It's not just about muscle, not that you lot have got much in that department.

TEAM 1: Excuse me!

TEAM 2: Speak for yourself, girlie.

BETTS: It's about tactics, deception and cunning. Us lot [*She points to self*] are good at that.

Shocked looks from team

TEAM 3: You mean?

BETTS: Yup. The girls' football team is amalgamating with the boys'!

TEAM 4: Amangarating?

TEAM 5: Amalgamazing?

TEAM 6: A magazine?

BETTS: Forgive me for the long words. I forgot that girls develop faster than boys…

TEAM 7: In all sorts of ways!

Boys laugh

Betts: To translate, for those with limited intelligence, I and a couple of my team-mates are joining up.

BOYS: [*Collective groan from boys*] You're joking! [*To Moley*] Tell us she's joking!

BETTS: Never been more serious.

MOLEY: That's that settled then. Jolly good. Lot of matches coming up, time for some serious training. Let Gregory and his little gang of losers get lost. We don't need them.

Exit, team members shrugging

Scene 12

This scene hurls insults between two opposing camps, Moley's new team and Gregory's gang of disgruntled former players, as though a mimed ball is being slammed between each side. Gang M is Moley's gang and Gang G is Gregory's. As the ball/insult lands each time, the other side sway back as if wounded/punched before recovering and throwing their own insult back.

GANG M: Ha. There they are! Three jeers for the team members who led the team all the way…to the bottom of the league!

GANG G: Oh ha ha! Your wit hit the crossbar and bounced right off. Don't come any closer, I'm allergic to incompetence!

GANG M: *[Turn to look at own gang members]* He says he's incontinent!

GANG G: Very funny. What a striking sense of humour. How long has it been on strike?

GANG M: If that insult was a ball, I'd say you're missing the other one!

ALL GANG G: Oooohhh!

GANG G: Face it, Moley, the only way you could get ahead is to borrow one.

GANG M: Poor Gregory, had a bad accident when he was young…being born.

GANG G: Dexter expects you to go places. As far as I'm concerned…the sooner the better!

GANG M: A box of matches could strike better than you!

GANG G: Oh yes? Well, the only dribbling you're good for would be in the loony bin!

GANG M: There is a cure for your lack of talent by the way: stop breathing!

GANG G: The only way you'll ever get near the net is hiding in your auntie's net curtains.

Betts enters. Stands with arms folded, shaking head. Gangs move closer until they're almost screaming in each other's faces

GANG M: Oh yeah?

GANG G: Yeah.

GANG M: Wanna make something of it?

GANG G: Does this look like Design and Technology?

GANG M: Right then. Outside! Now!

GANG G: *[Advance toward gang M]* We are outside!

GANG M: Mmmm. We knew that. *[Moley's gang are being slowly pressed up against the wall – ie they are the true cowards]* We'll do you!

GANG G: The only 'doo' will be the stuff we look forward to rubbing your faces in.

GANG M: *[Almost shrinking]* You're toast.

GANG G: And you're jam – the red stuff that oozes out of your bloody noses!

BETTS: *[Steps forward and blows whistle, holding up hand. Moves to stand between the two groups, pushing them apart]* Match over! Nil, nil morons! Honestly. Have we all forgotten who the real rivals are? Go on - SCRAM. *[Claps hands together sharply. All except Gregory scatter and scurry off, looking ashamed as Betts*

shoos them]
Sound of school bell
GREGORY: *[Forcefully]* Oh…Bells! She's right.
Exit

Scene 13

Enter Tim and Jim.

TIM: Well Jim, we've climbed a mountain,

JIM: and reached the summit of half time.

TIM: The view is not pretty.

JIM: In fact it's as ugly as a wart.

TIM: A hairy wart.

JIM: A hairy wart in a very embarrassing place.

TIM: A hairy wart in a very embarrassing place, which when you try to sit down on it,

BOTH: HURTS!

TIM: The school is in a bad way,

JIM: like a hamster in a washing machine.

TIM: Morale is low.

JIM: No leads on the thieves,

TIM: what with the team being all over the shop,

JIM: like shelves full of dodgy goods.

Both shake their heads

JIM: It could be a funeral.

TIM: It's not football as we know it, Jim.

JIM: Can Moley really carry it off?

TIM: Who knows.

JIM: Will Mrs Prodger win her evil match?

TIM: And do we really care?

JIM: And as for the cup?

TIM: *[Stands up]* It's well and truly gone, like my bladder will be if we don't get a break.

JIM: The people at home will enjoy that detail Tim.

TIM: My pleasure, Jim.

Exit

If breaking for a short interval, use next line to indicate the break

TIM AND JIM: Half time!

Act Two - Scene 1

Lights up on Moley, Betts and new team running round the stage in circles. Several are obviously not fit and out of breath.

BETTS: *[Clicks a stopwatch and shouts]* Stop!

MOLEY: Thanks Betts. OK Diddles, we could do better. Where we were is not where we are heading for. We need to look into ourselves. *[Pulls out mirror and admires himself]*

BETTS: What Moley means is that we need to find the strength inside. We can't blame anyone else.

MOLEY: You took the words out of my mouth, Betts. I think we should start with some, err…*[Looks to Betts]*

BETTS: Practice passes. Accurate ball placing is the key.

MOLEY: Exactly. I think you could be psychic, Betts!

Betts rolls her eyes. Various shouts of To me! To me! *as invisible ball is passed between team - and caught on feet, on chests, on heads and passed round the circle*

MOLEY: OK. Tactics. What went wrong in our last game?

Various shufflings of feet, coughs etc. No one answers

BETTS: Maybe we need to look at it again. Teamwork only gets us into the other half. It's what we do with the ball then that counts. Bouncing it off the crossbar just isn't good enough. Oh…sorry Moley. Didn't mean that personally.

MOLEY: *[Frowns]* No, not at all. Though I must say, perhaps if the ball had been passed to me properly, I would have scored. *[Glares at one of players]*

BETTS: So you don't mind talking us through it?

MOLEY: No...errr...why...not? So *[Remembering. Re-enacts]* Well, I had the ball, great control, up the pitch, ready to shoot...but oh, that water in my eyes - blinding for a moment. Hellish windy day, it was.

BETTS: Of course.

MOLEY: And I was just trying to flatten the grass first to get the perfect shot...

BETTS: Yup. OK. So, we all know what happened next. But let's just freeze it there shall we? Right, you. *[Indicates a player]* Goalkeeper. You two *[Indicates two players]* Goalposts! *[Betts now runs between Moley and 'goal', checking out the angles. She returns to Moley, alters his whole posture manually then bends down and adjusts his foot]*

BETTS: Good, now with a minor readjustment. Let's replay the fantasy version shall we?

Slow motion. Other team members spread out as though on pitch. This time as Moley kicks, he smiles. Goalie looks scared and mimes missing as imagined ball slips round his side into the net. Goalie puts hands to face, falls to knees and weeps. Victory hugs and gestures. Moley lifted on to shoulders of mates, before being finally being put down next to Betts. The ball can either be mimed, as indicated, or a performer wearing a 'football' hat can physically enact being the ball ie lying down with head by Moley's foot, jumping up to soar toward the goal and swerving round the side of the goalie in a forward roll to the back of the net!

MOLEY: That was...

BETTS: Brilliant. And with you *leading* us, we can turn over a new leaf.

MOLEY: I was thinking...

BETTS: Five sessions a week, every day after school.

MOLEY: And…

BETTS: No excuses, no whingeing, no complaints. Keep your eye on the ball at ALL times. Victory. Victory. Victory! There's no room for anything else!

MOLEY: Great. Carry on team.

Lights fade, as team jog round in circle again. Exit

Scene 2

Cheerleaders troop on. Through rhyme, chant and choreographed movement, they chart the turnaround in Diddlebury's football fortunes. If desired, Moley's team can also enact the matches in tableaux snapshots. Puns need to be emphasized by cheerleaders and rhythm needs to be spot on. Where words are indicated in capitals, each individual letter is spelt out. So, for example, the last 'K' of K-I-C-K will rhyme with 'day'.

CHEERLEADERS: We love the Diddles!
               D-I-D-D-L-E-S!
               Come on you Diddles!
               Finest players? Y-E-S!
               In only eight short weeks of time,
               there's been a truly splendid climb.
               The past is toast! There's no more blame,
               we have new victors in this game.

All that training, nerves on the pitch,
did they beat West Ham...Sandwich?
Ha! Ate them up and can you guess,
kicked their B-U-T-T-S!
Aston Vanilla, made a mistake,
goalie trembled like a frothy milkshake!
Betts aimed winning K-I-C-K
Diddle up the league, so make our day.
Mash 'em'! Fry 'em! Beaten, cruel,
cowards! Chicken! Liver...pool.
M-O-L don't ask mE Y *[ie why]*,
groovy feet, gotta watch him fly.
Betts is cookin'! Trouncing them.

Kick the enemy's B-U-M!

Time flies by...whee...eeee...eee! *[All pause as they*
synchronise following something invisible flying through
sky above heads from stage left to right]

Loud voice from off-stage: **SPLAT!**

CHEERLEADERS:This is a winning recipe!
Diddlebury Heights, we love you best.
You're heroes who will beat the rest.
D-I-D-D-L-E-S!
In with a chance? Oh, Y-E-S
Say Y-E-S, yeah Y-E-S
No longer in an M-E-S-S!

Exit

Scene 3

Head, alone on stage behind a desk, head in hands. Ghost of Arnold Poulten-Mole stands to side of stage then slowly walks round desk.

HEAD: Nearly the end of term. The forklift of the past will indeed carry us all away, and as Head, I can do nothing. Our team of lawyers have led a classic defense. In vain. Surely there's another way? The land for the school was handed over 'in perpetuity' to serve this community, and exercise both mind and body. So what if the papers never turned up? The good man, Mr Arnold Poulten-Mole the First, made his intentions quite clear.

Ghost nods

There is no justice anymore, only the grasping fingers of greed.

Ghost nods again

Everything he gave has been stolen - even his cup. Poor man. If only Arnold were here now, he could tell me where the deeds are and the school would be saved.

Arnold puts his hands on the Head's shoulders in commiseration

No. It's too late. *[Looks around stage slowly]* I shall miss the old place - the squeaky lino in the corridors, the way the stairs have worn with endless feet. Oh, there are some who think me pompous. But I did my best…and it wasn't good enough. As matters stand, come the end of the final match on the last day of term, that *woman* will get what is wrongfully hers. Whether we win or lose on the pitch, the game is well and truly…over.

Both exit

Scene 4

Chance encounter in corridor between Gregory and Moley, plus Betts. Moley tries to needle Gregory but is undermined by Betts' accusing glare and Gregory's genuine humbleness.

GREGORY: Hi Betts. Hello Moley.

MOLEY: What, you're talking to me again?

GREGORY: Don't start. I just wanted to say…

MOLEY: That you're jealous. I know. I would be too if I saw myself playing so brilliantly. It's hard to stomach when someone shines out like that.

BETTS: Excuse me! There are other members in the team, Moley.

MOLEY: Oh yes. Of course. When I said I, I meant 'we'…

BETTS: Sure you did.

GREGORY: No. I'm not jealous…I'm proud. Proud of you all and the way the team's turned round. I just wanted to wish you good luck this Friday.

MOLEY: I don't think we need your good wishes…*mate.*

BETTS: *[Stares at Moley]* Moley! Lay off.

MOLEY: *[Pouts]* Okay. Sorry! You're proud of us…Thanks…

Gregory: I mean it. You both work well together. Keep it up.

MOLEY: *[Warms to the praise]* Actually, you're totally right, for once. We're getting there. Never thought I'd turn this insignificant bunch of losers round.

Betts puts hands on hips, she's heard enough and stalks off

...With a bit of help from the girls, I suppose. I have a dream! Not only do I intend to lead the team to victory but in addition, the cup will be restored! You'll see. Glory, glory, glory!

GREGORY: The cup?

MOLEY: *[As if explaining to a child]* The Poulten and Mole's Potted Shrimp Cup.

GREGORY: How, exactly?

MOLEY: Well, for a start, we'll win!

GREGORY: And? That will bring back *a stolen* cup...how?

MOLEY: What? Oh. Er...Yes. I...well...what I meant...was *[Thinks frantically]*...that, we'll show those brutes that stealing a historic cup won't steal them the title. I meant 'the title'. Silly me. Got it, ah, confused. Cup? What cup? Ha ha...

GREGORY: *[Looks closely at Moley]* You suddenly seem pretty sure that it *was* Mill Spill who pinched it.

MOLEY: Well...I...it's OBVIOUS! That is, to anyone with a couple of brain cells to rub together. The theft was discovered just after they left! They even boasted about how they would 'lift the cup'. It's not exactly Darwin's theory of relativity...

GREGORY: Einstein

MOLEY: What?

GREGORY: Einstein's theory.

MOLEY: Oh, for goodness sake. Whoever!

GREGORY: [Frowns] Maybe.

MOLEY: [Agitated. Looks at watch suddenly] Gotta go. Late for training. [Exit]

GREGORY: [Watches Moley go] Hmmm. There's something here that smells off - and it's not me! I might try some sniffing around.

Exit

Scene 5

Meeting between Mrs Prodger and Dexter. Should be performed in shadowy light as they walk round stage.

DEXTER: I know I asked if we could meet privately, but I don't see why it has to be in the dark!

MRS PRODGER: [Purrs] But my dear Mr Deputy Dexter, this isn't dark, it's just a little low in the lighting department. [She takes his arm]

DEXTER: Ermmm....

MRS PRODGER: I had a little fall on my ankle. Ligaments are such tender things, you know. I hope you don't mind giving me some extra...support. I am but a frail female...[She swoons a little]

DEXTER: Well...of course...But what I really want to talk about is whether there's anything we can do...

MRS PRODGER: Oh, there's plenty *you* can do for me. A clever, capable chap like you. [*Runs finger down his arm*]

DEXTER: I want to get straight to the point. This business with the school. Can I ask you…?

MRS PRODGER: Oh, business, business, business. It's all you fellows think about. Busy this, busy that and busy the other. Whereas I, a full-grown, ardent, warm-hearted woman…believe in pleasure…**before**… business. [*She leans over as if to kiss him*]

DEXTER: [*Has bent down to tie shoelace so that she falls over. He straightens*] Quite…Why are you on the floor?

MRS PRODGER: Oh…I lost something. [*To audience, snarls*] My inheritance. [*Composes herself*] Tell me. This football league thingy. How's that young…what's his name? Paul…doing?

DEXTER: Who? Moley? I'm surprised you follow local sporting matters. Very well, as it happens. The team have powered up the league. They're in with a chance of the title again. Amazing turnaround! The school almost seems to have its old spirit back again. I'm delighted.

MRS PRODGER: Well isn't that sweet? [*Aside*] One pathetic gasp from the decomposing old whale before it sinks below the surface for very last time…

DEXTER: Anyway. Back to the subject in hand. I have a proposal.

MRS PRODGER: Oh! [*Flutters hands*] Do you really mean it…?

DEXTER: Not THAT sort of a proposal! Really! I'd like you to consider something.

Lights fade. Exit

Scene 6

Commentators.

TIM:	What's going on, Jim?
JIM:	The plot thickens,
TIM:	like gravy
JIM:	with lumpy bits.
TIM:	There's trouble stirring.
JIM:	Is it a recipe
TIM:	for catastrophe?
JIM:	But back to the game.
TIM:	Today's the day, up against...?
JIM:	No, I don't think we should strain the brains of the people out there.

Both stare out towards audience

TIM:	*[Winces and shakes head]* You're right, Jim, as always. IQs look a bit low.
JIM:	Lower than a limbo dancer, Tim?
TIM:	Lower than a limbo dancer...down a sewer.
JIM:	*[Shouts, as though to make audience jump]* Mill
TIM:	Spill! Have you been paying attention?
JIM:	But the moment the match is over,
TIM:	it's the final whistle.
JIM:	Mrs P,
TIM:	the not-so-great granddaughter

JIM: with her snarling pack of lawyers:

TIM: men, with faces as hard as diamond-tipped
          chainsaws,

JIM: and women who'd happily sell their children for a
          skinny latte

TIM: with a cinnamon dusting;

JIM: Mrs. P...gets the land, the school, the grounds,

TIM: lock, stock

JIM: and stinking barrel of fish-yness.

TIM: Any chance of a late substitution?

JIM: A surprise from the benches,

TIM: a hero to save us all?

JIM: Like Arthur,

TIM: King of the Britons!

JIM: Hope swells in our hearts

TIM: like a lovely pair of...

JIM: balloons.

Off stage, two balloons are popped, one after the other. Exit

Scene 7

The final. Any cast not playing the cheerleaders or teams are spectators/supporters. Cheerleaders enter and the two teams line up. As before, the cheerleaders' lines can convey the action through their reactions. Alternatively, it can be simultaneously enacted on stage by the teams through use of stylized mime or synchronized choreography.

CHEERLEADERS: She's lined them up in a 4-4-2
Tactics Betts! Oh we love U!
With a D-I-D-D-L-E-S
It's S-U-C-C-E-S-S!
Underline it, spell it yes,
S-U-C-C-E-S-S!
As for thuggish thieves, Mill Spill,
they're well and truly over the hill!

Pause as Mill Spill get ready to throw coin

Mill Spill move, they give a toss.
Flip that coin, Diddle's loss.
First half starts, but oh! What's this?
Holy Moley, look at that miss!

Moley tries to pass ball to team member but it goes to opposition

Terrible tackle, dispossess
Diddles in an M-E-S-S.

Mill Spill shoot for goal

Nip it, slip it, A to B,
They shoot that shot S-H-O-T!
Beauty! Belter! Bouncing ball!

Diddles must fiddle and take the fall.
Home team feel that misery
as it flies in the back of the N-E-T

Whistle blows. Half time. Mill Spill jeer and chant

MILL SPILL: One-nil! Mill Spill! One-nil! Mill Spill!

Cheerleaders exit. Both teams huddle round on opposite side of stage. Dexter runs on to give a pep talk

DEXTER: It's only half time. Still plenty of opportunities. Don't give yourself a hard time, Moley. It could have happened to anyone.

BETTS: What do you mean? *[To Moley]* Haven't you worked out that you're supposed to pass to your own team members?

MOLEY: *[Whining]* It's not my fault. The ball was soggy.

ALL: Ahhhh!

MOLEY: It was! But listen Mr Dexter, I just need to pop back to the changing room for a moment. I'll be right back. *[Exits]*

DEXTER: OK but make it snappy. *[Turns to team and ushers them towards back of stage, giving them a run down on tactics to try in the second half]*

Both teams should be right at back of stage miming half time activities. Spectators improvise comments about getting a drink/snack, alongside comments on the game so far, as they move quickly off stage. Moley enters, creeping along front of stage, looking suspicious, holding a kit bag. Gregory enters from other side, sees Moley but is not seen himself. He steps back so that he is visible to the audience but not to Moley. Voice of Mrs Prodger calls from off stage

MRS PRODGER: Paul! Paul, where are you?

Moley stops and turns his head back towards the voice then shakes his head and continues creeping forwards along front of stage and off the other side

Paul...

GREGORY: [*About to follow*] Why on earth is he coming out of Mill Spill's changing room? [*Exits, following*]

MOLEY: [*Enters, running towards team who turn and move centre stage*] Mr Dexter, everyone! Come quickly! I've discovered something! I was just getting my lucky socks from where I accidentally left them in the changing room Mill Spill are using and I saw it! It was poking out of one of their bags, the scoundrels!

Gregory enters behind Moley. Spectators rush back onto stage

DEXTER: Saw what, boy? What is the matter? It's nearly time for the second half.

GREGORY: Is this what you're talking about? [*Holds up a bag. Mill Spill turn to look*]

MILL SPILL TEAM MEMBER: Oi! That's mine, that is!

MOLEY: Er...How? [*Looks confused then recovers*]...Yes! Exactly! It belongs to one of them! [*Points*] And what's inside it? [*He grabs bag from Gregory. Reaches in and pulls out the Cup*]

Everyone gasps and reacts

ALL: The Poulten and Mole's Potted Shrimp Cup!

HEAD: [*Steps forward and takes the cup*] Found! Returned to us! [*Face darkens*] Stolen [*Points to Mill Spill*] by these pilfering, purloining villains! The match must be stopped immediately! Mill Spill have brought dishonour on themselves.

MILL SPILL TEAM MEMBER: What? Lies! Nothing to do with me.

That is NOT on that is...

GREGORY: *[Has had arms folded all the time]* I agree. But why don't we ask Moley? He seems very keen to tell us all something.

MOLEY: I...yes...well, as I said, I had to go to find...to find...

GREGORY: *[Prompts]* Your lucky socks?!

MOLEY: My lucky socks, that's right, for the second half. Only, while I was looking to see where I'd left them, I fell over a bag and there it was - poking out! I bet they were planning to taunt us with it when the game was over. Only now they can't because, like Mr Stern said the game *is* over, isn't it?

MILL SPILL: Now wait a minute...

HEAD: Absolutely, I couldn't think of allowing it to continue. Moley my boy, you're the hero of the day. You have indeed returned the cup...

GREGORY: Excuse me Mr Stern, before we go any further, you might like to know what I saw...

MOLEY: *[Butts in, looking terrified]* You? Saw? Don't listen to him...

HEAD: *[Irritated]* What is it Gregory? Do hurry up.

GREGORY: He was in Mill Spill's changing room. I know because I followed him.

MOLEY: No! He's lying...

GREGORY: And the cup WAS in that bag -

Moley sighs with relief

... but only because Moley had just put it in there!

HEAD: What is the meaning of this?

MOLEY: Oh, I get it. Jealousy! Simple jealousy. Lousy captain, kicked off the team! What does he do to retaliate? He nicks the cup! Then he waits until the very last match to plant it on Mill Spill himself and seize the glory for 'finding' it. Only I found it first. So then what does he do? Tries to frame me! ME! The finest player this motley crew have had the privilege of...

BETTS: Actually, Moley old mate, I hate to point this out, but the cup was nicked *before* Gregory was chucked out of the team.

MOLEY: [*Starts backing away*] Yeah...so...he...planned it in advance? Or...or...he saw it in Mill Spill's bag, just like I did, but he decided to set me up...or ‑

BETTS: Or perhaps you were so scared of losing the match, of losing face, that you took steps to make sure there wouldn't *be* a second half? That's neat: 'hero of the day' without scoring a goal!

GREGORY: Just one more little question, *PAUL*. What was your mother doing here?

MOLEY: [*Squeaks*] Mother?

GREGORY: 'No one calls me Paul except my mum.' Remember?

MOLEY: Oh...so? She's in...Spain.

Mrs Prodger strides on

MRS PRODGER: Oh, for goodness' sake darling. We can surely drop the pretence now?

All gasp

After all, if the match *is* over then I do believe that ...oh yes! All you people are now TRESPASSING on MY property! And while we're about it, I might as well have that too. [*She grabs cup*] I'm sure it's technically mine, what with it bearing the name of my estimable relative! [*Turns to Moley. Hisses*] Really Paul, what were you thinking of? Just because 'borrowing' the darned thing didn't help us to track down those papers before anyone else found them and ruined our claim, it didn't mean you needed to give it back. It's still worth a mint!

HEAD: [*Grabs the other side of the cup and holds on*] How dare you! You stole the cup? *That* belongs to the school. Get your filthy paws off!

MRS PRODGER: [*She holds on tightly*] 'Stole'? Paul just took what I regarded as rightfully mine.

Cast react to this news by turning threateningly towards Moley

MOLEY: What are you saying? I thought we weren't going to let on?

HEAD: It is NOT yours!

MRS PRODGER: It is now! Anyway what good is it to you? I found an ancient diary of Arnold's. It said that clues in the inscription on this blasted cup would 'provide a key to where the deeds are hidden'. What a load of old piffle! Silly codger must have been senile. My son has managed to search every square centimetre of this place. There are no papers. There probably never were.

MOLEY: No! I didn't! Well, I did, but she put me up to it.

MRS PRODGER: [*Ignores Moley*] Let go, blast you!

HEAD: No!

Tug of war ensues. All watch in horror

HEAD: You...let...go-o-o...oof...

Sudden bang and base of cup flies apart. Set of papers falls out and flutters to the ground. Mrs Prodger dives for them but falls

MRS PRODGER: NOoooo.

MOLEY: *[Calling for help because he is surrounded]* Mum!

MRS PRODGER: Shut up, you stupid, stupid boy and help me. *[She tries to reach the papers, but Dexter runs forward and makes a fantastic dive and forward roll for them, scooping them up before she can do anything]*

CHORUS MEMBER: What a tackle! Didn't know he had it in him!

MRS PRODGER: Mr Dexter! My dear Mr Dexter, remember our little chat?

DEXTER: Ah yes. Our little chat! That would be the one when I finally got a word in edgeways to ask you, very honourably, to think of the local community and to drop your claim on the school, would it? *[Hands papers to Head]* The same little chat where you told me you'd rather go snorkeling in a pool of liquid manure?

HEAD: *[Scanning the papers]* Ah! I see! Good old Arnold! Well now, there's bad deeds…*[Stares at Mrs Prodger, sitting on floor in disarray]* and there's good deeds and this, dear friends, is a set of very good deeds indeed! 'All yours'? *[To Mrs Prodger]* I think not!

He reads and ghost of Arnold walks on, reading alongside him until it is Arnold speaking and not the Head

I, Arnold Poulten-Mole the First, hereby bequeath the land on which shall stand a fine new school and all the grounds surrounding it, in perpetuity and for ever more to be kept in the control of the governing body and head teacher, whomsoever that may be, that Diddlebury Heights may ascend the heights of true sportsmanship. Signed and witnessed this day of our lord, 13th April, 1931.

59

All freeze. Chorus move, splitting into two groups, so that the facts are explained like a ball being tossed from side to side. Other performers, as crowd, turn heads from side to side like a tennis match

CHORUS 1: So that means

2:      Yes?

1:      That the proof has been found!

2:      Yes!

1:      The school is saved!

2:      Yes

1:      Just in the nick of time?

2:      Yes!

1:      And that explains the inscription on the cup: 'It shall stand for all time as a record of *good deeds*!'

2:      Yes! Can we say more than 'Yes'?

1:      No. And Mrs Prodger was trying to find the deeds and destroy them?

2:      Yes!

1:      So she sent her son in disguise to the school?

2:      Yes!

1:      Mrs Prodger, born Poulten-Mole?

2:      Yes!

1:      Hence Moley's nickname? What a sneaking, two-faced spy!

2:      Yes!

1:      And Dexter didn't nick it? And he was never in league with Mrs P.?

2:      No! Ha! Caught you!

1:      Damn. And Mill Spill were too thick to even think of nicking it!

2:      Yes.

1:      They were red herrings!

2:      Yes!

1:      Are herrings red?

2:      Yes! (Actually, we don't know.)

1:      What happens next? Can we get on with the game!

2:      All right then.

HEAD: My dear Mrs Prodger and young Paul. Please allow me to arrange for your escort to somewhere quieter where you can await the arrival of the police.

Head takes charge of arranging for Mrs Prodger and Moley to be dragged off. Mother and son protest innocence. Moley repeats his claims that it was all her idea and nothing to do with him: he was only following her orders. Head waits until they are off stage before continuing

And now, I believe we still have a second half to attend to.

Spotlight on commentators

JIM: Well Tim, never seen anything like it.

TIM: There were more twists

JIM: than a boa constrictor

TIM: with gut ache.

JIM: Moley and his evil mother are stretchered off to be locked in the head's study and the team's without a captain.

TIM: Like a man without any clothes,

JIM: streaking across the pitch.

TIM: It's not a pretty sight!

JIM: This is going to leave the team in a bit of a pickle.

TIM: But what's this? Betts is conferencing with the Deputy

JIM: and Gregory is shaking his head.

TIM: Betts punches him

JIM: hard…and now he's nodding his head.

TIM: The whistle goes,

JIM: like a steam train

TIM: and, I don't believe it, Gregory puffs on.

JIM: The crowd goes wild – they're

TIM: Chuff, chuff, chuffed!

Whistle goes. Cheerleaders step forward

CHEERLEADERS: Here's the man we want to see!
Check out the buns on Gregory!
What a kick, it's rhythm and rhyme
Sprints like a cheetah on double time.

GREGORY: [*Shouts*] To me! To me!

CHEERLEADERS: Lovely cross, wheeee!
Gets it. Goalie does a spread,
Doesn't know it, but he's dead!
Yes dead with D-E-A and D
Scored by the Guy with Ener-G
Mill Spill, thick as wooden planks,
Lumbering around like tanks
Poor old goalie sinks like a rock
As the team is suffering – shellshock!

And now we're into extra time.
Will it be a draw? No! Got to climb
All the way to the T-O-P
Change the line up 3-4-3
Touch, tap, take the cross,
Baby Betts now she's the boss.
Close the gap as we sing on the mike
Bet on the ball with a super strike.
Who said girls with curly locks
Can't play it, play it, in the box?
Watch that dainty foot connect,
She sinks the ball, they are
SHIP-WRECKED!

Crowd go wild, jump up and down, run round stage, cheering and whistling then miming as commentators finish

JIM: Oh my, oh my, oh my, Tim.

TIM: I'm not yours, Jim.

JIM: It's amazing, stupendous. I'm stuck for words,

TIM: like a hand

JIM: down a blocked sewage pipe.

TIM: They've covered themselves in glory,

JIM: like a shower of vanilla ice cream,

TIM: with a chopped nut topping

JIM: and cream - to whip Mill Spill good and proper.

TIM: They've got the cup!

JIM: And they've won the cup!

TIM: The school has been returned,

JIM: like a lost teddy

TIM: to its owner. [*Takes out teddy and puts it on stand*]

JIM: Thanks Tim.

TIM: It's a pleasure Jim.

JIM: Mrs Prodger will inherit a plot

TIM: six foot by seven foot wide,

JIM: with bars on the windows.

TIM: Moley will be sent to a highly distant aunt,

JIM: who hates children,

TIM: especially spoiled, uppity gits who think the sun shines out of their -

JIM: as-k me, he's in for trouble.

TIM: And the ghost of Arnold Poulten-Mole will be home at last

JIM: like a spatula in a cutlery drawer.

TIM: This is truly

JIM: a good result!

END

Rehearsal and Workshop ideas

Ways in

1. Physical reactions are important for creating comedy in this play. This exercise demands exaggerated facial expressions and gestures to communicate the reactions of groups of spectators watching a football match. In small groups, improvise a range of responses to watching an imagined match where
   a) The home team score
   b) The away team score (twice)
   c) A foul is committed
   d) There's a penalty
   e) There's a disturbance on the pitch.
   No words are allowed – only mime. Aim to communicate feelings as well as immediate responses to what is happening on the pitch. When showing each group's performance, freeze moments of the action and comment on what the facial expressions tell the audience.

2. There are a number of stage directions in *Kick Off* for using a sequence of tableaux to show fragments of action. Tableaux are also known as freeze-frames or still-lifes and are intended to present a frozen picture on stage. Using the following list, in small groups, devise a single tableau for each heading. Then, repeat each heading but devise three linked tableaux which show three stages of, for example, being relieved.

EXHAUSTED	TERRIFIED
HORRIFIED	RELIEVED

IMPATIENT	IN PAIN
DICTATORIAL	WORRIED
ASHAMED	LOATHING
PLEASED	TRIUMPHANT
ASTONISHED	JEALOUS
WINNERS	LOSERS

3. Move on from creating single or triple tableaux to creating a comic strip. The pictures should link to tell a story. Always be aware of where the focal point is in each picture.
   Ideas:
   a) A confrontation. Create 6 tableaux leading to the point just *before* physical conflict erupts
   b) An accident. Create between 5 and 10 pictures
   c) A football match shown from the point of view of the players on the pitch, using the same 5 events suggested in number 1 above

4. Exaggerated movement and body language are also required for performing some of the more cartoon-like characters in *Kick Off*, such as the Head Teacher and Mrs Prodger. Begin with developing exaggerated walks for two extreme character types: royalty and servants. Walk around the space as though you are either a king or queen. Think about how to hold your head, how you lift your knees, how you hold your shoulders, where your hands are placed. Repeat as a newly appointed, nervous servant.

Status

1. The status that each character has (or thinks s/he has) is crucial to his/her relationships with other characters. Status is revealed in many ways. One of the most obvious and

important is in the use of eye-contact. As a whole group, walk around the space without making any eye-contact at all.

Divide the group in half. Group 1 must seek eye-contact and hold it directly for a moment before moving on. Group 2 must break eye-contact and look down the moment someone meets their eye. Swap the groups around and repeat. Discuss how it felt at each stage of the exercise. How was high status shown?

2. In Act 1, Scene 1, the high status of the Head Teacher is very clear because he is addressing an assembly of pupils. The power relationship is easy: the Head has the highest authority as boss and the pupils are (supposed to be) subservient. However, in Act 1, Scene 3 with the Head Teacher and the Deputy Head, the Head's authority is subtly challenged and undermined and there are shifts in the power relationship. As a prelude to working on this scene, try 2 versions of the master and servant exercise. In pairs, decide who is master and who is the servant.

a) The master gives a series of orders which the servant responds to in a meek and totally compliant way.

b) The master gives orders, as before. However, this time, the servant 'appears' to be meek but comes up with all sorts of reasons why the orders can't be done or fulfilled. Who has the upper hand? Comment on how status is shown each time.

Character development

1. The characters of the Head Teacher, Mrs Prodger and Mr/s Patterson are all caricatures. Each role demands a quite exaggerated performance style for successful comic effect.

Choose one of these roles and work on a physical performance of this character, without speaking. Run through a sequence of actions from sitting, standing, walking, dressing, to walking up to someone for the first time to greet them. Finally, in a circle, take it in turns to enter the circle in role and to introduce yourself, staying in character.

2. Choose one of the characters above, then choose a scene in which they appear. Without speaking the text, work on non-verbal communication to convey the gist of the scene, concentrating especially on posture, facial expression, mannerisms and gestures.

   Comment on what you notice about how you move as each character. For example, you many find that the role of the Head Teacher uses a very upright posture, lots of shoulder and arm movements and searching eye-contact. The role of Mrs Prodger is led from the head, neck and nose, with her limbs and body moving in a languid but predatory, snake-like way, whereas Patterson's movements are stiffened, jerky, and fluttering, involving a lot of small hand movements and nervous mannerisms.

3. In role as either Betts or Gregory, write and perform a monologue revealing your thoughts and responses after Moley has been made team captain.

4. Take it in turns to hot-seat each other in role as either Betts, Gregory or Moley, just before the final match. Ask questions about feelings and reactions in particular. Concentrate as much on how each character communicates, using posture, facial expression and gesture, as on what they actually say.

5. Choose any of the main, named characters. Much mechanical action happens on stage because performers are concerned more with getting their lines said than with presenting a whole picture. The words we have written in this play are only a part of the jigsaw that will make a final picture. Developing a character for performance is like pumping air into a balloon. Expand and fill the character with its own life!

   This exercise concentrates on purposeful action. Decide what sort of bag your character would use and carry. Make a list of what you think should be in it and why. Choose a few lines or a short section of speech from anywhere in the play. Perform this short speech. Perform this short piece whilst either carrying, fiddling with or looking in your bag. Does this help you to focus on what your character is <u>doing</u> as well as saying?

Improvisation

Improvise the scene between Mrs Prodger and Paul 'Moley', her son, before the beginning of the play where Mrs Prodger persuades him to go to Diddlebury Heights in order to attempt to find (and destroy) the deeds.

Performing the text

1. Jim and Tim (or Queenie and Jeannie) are intended to work as a comedy double-act. However, it is possible to re-allocate the lines to a group of 3 or even four. Experiment with different ways of chopping up and allocating the lines. How does it alter the effect? Performing the commentators' roles in this way requires the group to work very closely as though they are all plugged into the same brain or computer

programme. (If you do decide to perform these roles with more than two people, then extra, rhyming names need to be added – such as Finn or Reenie).

2. The characters of Jim and Tim (or Queenie and Jeannie) rely on comic timing. Practise their scenes at different speeds to gauge their effect on an audience. Do one of the scenes quickly, without any pauses before the puns, and then repeat with pauses added in. Discuss the difference. In pairs, make up your own commentator scenes based on observing a football match, a car race, a tennis match, a gymnastic competition, a snowboarding competition. Try to come up with outlandish/strange/bizarre similes.